Wrapped Up In A Hitta's Love for Christmas

NAI

URBAN AINT DEAD

Email: urbanaintdead@gmail.com

Print ISBN: 979-8-9906748-9-9

Contents

Also by Nai — 7
Stay Up to Date — 9
Soundtracks — 11
Urban Aint Dead — 13
Submissions — 15

1. Hasan — 17
2. Charisma — 27
3. Hasan — 39
4. Charisma — 49
5. Hasan — 59
6. Charisma — 67
7. Charisma — 79
8. Hasan — 89
9. Charisma — 99
   Epilogue — 109

The End — 113
Review — 115
Also by Nai — 117
Other Books By — 119
Coming Soon — 123
Books By — 125
Stay Connected — 127

Also by Nai

Bossin' Up On The Plug

Bossin' Up On The Plug 2

In The Trenches With My Hitta

In The Trenches With My Hitta 2

Stealing A Queenpin's Heart

Stealing A Queenpin's Heart 2

A Piece of A Hustler's Heart

A Piece of A Hustler's Heart 2

A Thug's Love Mended My Heart

A Thug's Love Mended My Heart 2

A Summer To Remember With My New York Bae

A Summer Fling In New York

His Hood Love Gave Me Life

His Hood Love Gave Me Life 2

My Thug, My Sanctuary

Thug Kisses For Christmas

For The Love Of My Savage

Charge It To The Game

Charge It To The Game 2

A Summer To Remember With My Hitta

Snatched Up By A Hitta

Santa Sent Me A Real One For Christmas

Wet Dreams On Lockdown: The Unit Manager

Thug Me The Right Way

Thug Me The Right Way 2

Thug Me The Right Way 3

Seizing A Gangsta's Heart For The Summer

Yours For The Taking

Stay Up to Date

To stay up to date on new releases, plus get information on contests, sneak peaks and more,
Click the link below...
https://mailchi.mp/6d21003686d1/subscribe

<u>**Soundtracks**</u>

Scan the QR Code below to listen to the Soundtracks/Singles
of some of your favorite U.A.D titles:

Don't have Spotify or Apple Music?
No Sweat!
Visit your choice streaming platform and search URBAN
AINT DEAD.

Currently on lock serving a bid?
JPay, iHeartRadio, WHATEVER!
We got you covered.

Simply log into your facility's kiosk or tablet, go to music and
search URBAN AINT DEAD.

Urban Aint Dead

Like & Follow us on social media:
FB - URBAN AINT DEAD
IG: @urbanaintdead
Tik Tok - @urbanaintdead

Submissions

Submit the first three chapters of your completed manuscript to urbanaintdead@gmail.com, subject line: Your book's title. The manuscript must be in a .doc file and sent as an attachment. The document should be in Times New Roman, double-spaced, and in size 12 font. Also, provide your synopsis and full contact information. If sending multiple submissions, they must each be in a separate email. Have a story but no way to submit it electronically? You can still submit to URBAN AINT DEAD. Send in the first three chapters, written or typed, of your completed manuscript to:

URBAN AINT DEAD
P.O Box 448
Maybrook, NY 12543

DO NOT send original manuscript. Must be a duplicate.
Provide your synopsis and a cover letter containing your full contact information.
Thanks for considering URBAN AINT DEAD.

Hasan

"Oh, my Goddd, bae! Can you please come and help me with these boots?"

The frustration in Charisma's voice was evident as she called out to me. I knew that if I didn't come to her aid immediately, the tears wouldn't be too far behind. We were in the third trimester of her pregnancy, and my baby was a ball of emotions.

"Here I come, baby." Grabbing her Stanley cup full of ice water, I took the steps two at a time and entered our bedroom. "Awww, Big Mama. I was tryna make it here before you started crying. Come on, gimme your foot."

Seated on the edge of the bed in a sweater dress, her hair in a low ponytail that hung to the middle of her back and light makeup, she was beautiful. Charisma was bad when we met, but our baby had given her a glow that was hard to miss.

Fanning her face to stop the tears that pooled in the corners of her eyes, she hit the bed.

"This is dumb, Hasan. I just wore these boots last month, and they fit fine. Everything is swelling. And I..." She paused and sucked in a breath.

"There you go. Now breathe out slowly and relax. I got you." I had learned her emotional meter over the last eight and a half months, and she wasn't at the point of a complete breakdown — yet.

"I don't even wanna go no more." She pouted.

"Whatever you wanna do, bae. It's not that deep. We can stay home."

She'd persuaded me that we needed another photoshoot that included Bella since she missed the maternity shoot we'd done two weeks ago. From day one, Charisma stressed the importance of Bella being a part of the pregnancy, and I appreciated that. At no point did she want her to feel left out.

"We can't. We already told Bells we were coming to get her. You know we can't go back on our word. Here." She held her foot up and wiped her eyes. "Let's do this."

"I thought these were the boots you said shorty said y'all burnt out." I held the boot up to examine it.

"Yeah, Latto did say that. And I don't give a damn cause these boots weren't cheap."

I laughed at the frown on her face and commenced to sliding them on her feet without hassle. Once they were both on, I pulled her up from the bed and kissed her nose. "So, you ain't listenin' to Latto no more?"

"I ain't say all that." She giggled.

"You good now?"

"Yes. I'm good. I'll be even better if you put your lips on mine."

"Which ones?" I teased seriously.

"You so nasty. Get your mind out the gutter."

"I can't help it, Ma. You so damn fine." Turning her around so that she faced the floor length mirror in the corner of our bedroom, I wrapped my arms around her waist, rubbing her belly.

"I can't believe we're two weeks away from our due date. It's crazy to think we'll have another little one running around here soon."

I thought about what she said and nodded at her revelation. We'd come a long way over the last few months. The early days of her pregnancy were a blend of excitement and uncertainty. As we navigated the first trimester, it helped us realize what we needed from one another to make the transition to parenthood as easy as possible.

"Hasan, I'm scared," Charisma confessed, as she laid in my arms with her back facing me. Her voice was low —_as if she didn't want me to hear the words she spoke.

Her admission was real and a fact that I knew she grappled with. I could tell by how cautious she'd been daily since telling me she was pregnant. I wanted to turn her around but figured she didn't want to be seen in her vulnerable state, so I pulled her back to me instead. Kissing the back of her neck, I placed my hands on her belly.

"It's okay to be scared. You can be scared with me, 2A. So long as you know I got you and our baby, you can be as scared as you wanna be. You're my responsibility now."

Not only were we going through a pregnancy together, but we were also dating each other throughout the process. Watching her bravely face the challenges of pregnancy while fully embracing the beginning stages of motherhood only made my feelings grow stronger for her. While I'd experienced the full nine months of pregnancy with Heather, we didn't have the closeness that I'd developed with Charisma.

"I'm so tired of throwing up. I wanna enjoy my food at least once without racing to the bathroom before I can even digest it." Shifting in the bed, she turned so that she was now facing me. "What you smiling at?"

Leaning forward, I kissed her lips. "I really put a baby in you."

Nodding, she smiled back. "Yes, you did. Don't know the first thing about the pull-out method."

"You try sticking your fingers in that wet box and see how she sucks you in. It'll make sense then."

"You so nasty." Punching my arm playfully, she shook her head. "Seriously though. I'm gonna do my best to not project my fears on you and take things one day at a time. I know you're tired of hearing me complain. We still have months to go."

"I'm not tired of you speaking your truth. I'm also not trippin' bout you throwing up every hour on the hour. Whatever you need, I'ma be here to make the process as smooth as possible. That includes having a healthy and safe environment for you to be

scared in. Know that you can speak your fears because the moment I lined your womb with my seed, this became an us thing."

She stared at me silently, and I watched as her chest rose and fell while tears trickled down her face. Reaching up and rubbing the scar under my eye, she kissed me. I wasn't a sentimental nigga by any sense of the word unless it had something to do with Bells, but the emotion that Charisma displayed in this moment made my heart do silly shit. Placing one hand on her belly and the other on her chest, I sent a prayer up to God for a safe pregnancy and for our relationship to remain solid.

"You still not nervous?" she questioned, bringing me back to the present.

"Nope. I'm ready for baby number two."

"What if the baby comes on Christmas day?"

"Double the gifts."

Turning back to face me, she smoothed out my Lacoste sweater with a grin. "You still wanna wait to find out the gender?"

"Nah. You the only one that wants to be surprised. And you swore our doctor to secrecy. What you bribe that lady with anyway? The last two appointments, she ain't budge when I asked the gender. I'm like, 'Damn, Dr. Clarke, you a part of B16 or something?'"

"She is. And I'm Olivia Pope. She knows better."

"Maann, please. I think it's a princess in there. I can tell by how high your stomach sittin'. When Heather..." I paused when I noticed her scrunched up face. "What?"

"Please don't do that."

"Do what?"

"Compare me to your other baby mama. I don't care to know about her experience."

"Respect. My bad."

"It's okay. I'm not mad. It's just... you know."

"I get it, bae."

"Thanks for understanding." Glancing down at her watch, she looked back up at me. "We should get going before we're late."

"Cool."

Grabbing our coats from the closet, I helped her into hers before putting on mine. The winter was vicious around this time, and I found myself having to almost bully Charisma into wearing a hat and scarf, reminding her that I didn't give a damn about a leave out or a weave out. She wasn't about to be sick on my watch because she was trying to be cute. Holding out the hat and scarf set I'd picked up for her from the Gap, she sucked her teeth.

"Baeeee, my hair," she whined.

"Baeeee, I don't careee," I mimicked her whining, making her snatch the hat and scarf from me. Chuckling, I watched as she put them both on, careful not to disturb her ponytail.

"Happy?"

"Very."

Taking her hand in mine, I guided her out the front door and to the car. Securing her in the passenger seat, I got in on the driver's side. Falling into our usual routine when we drove together, she connected her phone to the car, selected the car playlist she'd created, and held out her hand for me to hold. Since making it official, I'd come to know Charisma inside and out. She'd made it a requirement that we still dated each other throughout the pregnancy. In that time of courting her, I'd learned so much, not just about her but about myself.

2A had a nigga doing love language tests and shit I never thought I'd do. Yet, here I was, ready to be that guy for her while still remaining myself. Some said different women brought out different things in a man. My woman created a space where I could love her the way she needed without compromising who I was at heart — a street nigga. She not only accepted that, but she embraced it.

"Ooouuu, bae. I just added this song the other day. Listen. *Hey, how you doing? How's ya day going? You know that you can always say what's on your mind. Are you on your way home? I'll warm up yo' plate when you arrive.*"

"That's Ella Mai?"

She smiled and nodded.

"You love a nigga, huh?"

"I do."

"I like the way those two words sound together."

"Oh, hush." She giggled. "Did you let Heather know we were on our way?"

"Yeah. Bells should be dressed by the time we get there. I'll text again though."

Knowing Heather didn't miss an opportunity to do some shit to blow me, I sent her a text letting her know we'd be to her in forty-five minutes. Lately, she'd been doing her best to make coparenting difficult for me. And honestly, if it wasn't for Charisma reminding me that I had to keep an open line of communication for Bella, her silly ass would've been blocked. I had no problem going through a third party to get Bells if it came down to it.

Since finding out about Charisma's pregnancy, Heather had been vocal about how quickly our relationship had developed and questioned if Charisma had an ulterior motive. She even went as far as to say it was selfish of me to have impregnated another woman when Bella was still in the toddler stage. Why she thought she had a hold on my sperm because she gave birth to my first born was insane to me. On more than one occasion, I found myself having to remind her that her role was Bella's mother. I didn't need her policing shit I had going on.

"I can't wait to see Bells in the dress we got her. These pictures are gonna be so cute."

"You said you hired a makeup artist, right?"

"Yeah. It came with the package. Why?"

"I just wanna make sure when the waterworks get started, there's someone there to get you right. I can't do no makeup, bae. And have no desire to."

"Hasan. It's not even that bad."

"Baby, I love you but come on now. Just last night, you cried because one of the grilled cheese sandwiches I made you was darker than the other."

With what I now referred to as the pregnant pout etched on her face, she replied. "They didn't taste the same."

"If you say so. But didn't I get up and make you two new ones?" She nodded. "And didn't you still cry?" She nodded again, this time with a smile.

"I cried cause I was grateful. That was sweet of you."

"Yo cap ass. You cried because you spoiled. And that's okay. Between you, Bella, and the new princess coming, I'ma need another me."

Arriving at Heather's place, I lucked up on a parking spot in front of the building. Unbuckling her seatbelt, Charisma leaned over as much as her belly would allow and kissed my lips softly.

"You want me to kiss the other you like that?"

"And make me a single father of two? I'd hate to have to raise our baby alone because your lips had a mind of their own."

"Did you just threaten a pregnant woman?"

"No. I made a promise to **my** pregnant woman." She clamped her lips shut, making me laugh. "That's what I thought. Come on so we're not late."

I went to step out of the car, and she stopped me. "I'm gonna stay in the car, bae. I'll be moving around a lot once we get to the shoot, and I wanna stay off my feet as much as possible."

"So, you want me to carry you? You know damn well I'm not leaving you down here by yourself."

"Hasan, really? You're gonna be in and out."

"Exactly." Pushing my door open, I got out and walked over to her side to open her door. "So, am I carrying you, or you wanna walk?"

"I can walk, crazy man." Using my arm to help pull herself

up, she got out. "Hasan, I don't want any drama today. Let's just get Bella and be on our way."

"Heard." I couldn't say anything more than that. There was no telling what type of time Heather would be on. All I knew was that I wasn't going to let it affect my woman or disrupt the day she had planned.

Charisma

Walking hand in hand with Hasan, I mentally prepared myself for an exchange of words between me and Heather. Though we hadn't had any face to face run ins, I'd overheard her on the phone with Hasan, throwing dirt on my name more than once. Now, given my track record and vicious way with words, I could've torn into her, but with a man like Hasan, I never had to. The way he stepped behind me let me know that I was more than covered when I wasn't in his presence. Besides, I'd be the crazy one if I argued with a bitch that had a brain the size of a kidney bean.

I did my best to be the girlfriend who knew boundaries. I didn't overstep when it came to Bella, and I made sure that Hasan kept an open line of positive communication. We didn't start having an issue until she found out about the baby. And the beef was very much one sided. It was clear that my pregnancy had solidified things and put an official stamp on our relationship, further letting her know that I wasn't going anywhere —_not that Hasan would let me anyway.

The way this man doted on me daily was something out of a movie. Each morning, I woke up to tender kisses on my lips, a kiss to my belly, and a verbal reminder that we were doing this thing together —_or as he would say, *"We doin' this shit, 2A."* He was gentle with me when I cried for the silliest things and strong when I second guessed myself on the journey of motherhood. As our baby grew within me, so did our love — a love that neither of us saw coming but were mindful in how we perfected it.

From the little flutters to full on kicks, our little one was a testament to the life we were creating together. And while Hasan anticipated my every need and reassured me, I made sure to show him how much I appreciated him. Though pregnancy had me down for the first trimester, I still showed up for my man. Whether that was a listening ear, an available throat, or something wet for him to slide in, I made myself available. He didn't require much. Just the fact that I opened my eyes everyday and took a breath was more than enough for him. And those were his words, not mine.

"You good?" he questioned as we stepped off the elevator on Heather's floor.

"Mmhmm."

"Why you squeeze my hand then?"

You see. The man was in tune with me. "I'm okay, baby. Seriously."

"Okay." Reaching Heather's door, he knocked twice. There was no answer at first, prompting him to knock again. This time, a little harder.

"Who is it?" Heather called out from the other side.

"Bella's father."

I nudged him. "Bae."

"What? Am I not Bella's father?"

Before I could respond, the door opened to Heather's face which held a pleasant smile until she noticed me. Not easily offended, I kept my poise demeanor but didn't speak. All pleasantries aside, I'd mop the bottom of the ocean before I spoke to a bitch first that I knew held secret animosity toward me.

"Hey. I didn't know y'all were gonna come up to get her." She finally spoke, sounding dumb.

I'd already peeped her cryptic statement. What she really wanted to do was question why I was at her door in the first place.

"Would you have rather we'd told you to send Bella downstairs?" Hasan questioned to which she responded with an eye roll. "Is my baby dressed?"

"Yeah. Let me get her." Leaving the door slightly ajar, she walked off.

"Did she just leave us standing in the hallway?" Hasan spoke aloud but more so to himself.

I wasn't the least bit shocked. I didn't expect to be offered a seat. "This is why I should've stayed in the car. We could've avoided this."

"Charisma, I can fix this shit right now. I'll walk right in here, grab one of them chairs from her kitchen, and sit you in it. You know I give no fucks. All you gotta say is you're uncomfortable."

Picturing him acting on his statement made me giggle. The petty part of me wanted to use my pregnancy card and fake like my back was hurting, but I thought better of it.

"Go show Daddy your pretty dress, Bells."

Hearing Heather coach Bella toward the door, I got excited. I'd searched high and low to find a dress similar to mine for the photoshoot. It wasn't an easy feat at all. When Hasan noticed the stress settling in, he immediately got on the phone to enlist the help of my girls. And like I knew they would, Brae'lynn and Asani came through, finding the perfect dress in two days.

"Let Daddy see the princess," Hasan said as her little hand pressed against the door to pull it open. "I got it, Bells. Step back."

"Daddy, dress," she let out once he had the door fully open.

My brows dipped, and I clenched my fist. Seeing Bella twirl around in a completely different dress than the one I was sure Hasan had dropped off had me livid. He must've felt my mood shift because he gave me a look that said, *I got you*. I didn't want Heather to know she'd gotten under my skin, so I straightened my posture.

"Can we come inside?" he asked to which Heather hesitantly nodded.

"Wow, pretty girl," I finally spoke, doing my absolute best to not let Bella feel the tension. "Let me see you." She twirled her way over to me in a dress that looked like she was going to a beauty pageant and not a photoshoot. "You look so nice. You ready to take pictures?"

Nodding, she placed her hand on my belly and kissed it. "My baby," she proclaimed, making me smile.

"Ay, where the dress I dropped off here the other day?" Hasan questioned Heather, who was standing off to the side with the screw face.

"Daddy, dress," Bella repeated, her three-year-old mind clueless as to the switch that had me boiling inside.

"I know, baby. You look beautiful, but we're gonna put another dress on for the pictures. Right?" He glanced over at Heather, who shook her head.

"I didn't like the way the other dress fit," she said.

"Good thing you didn't buy it, and I don't need your permission to put it on her. Now, can you go get it? We got shit to do."

"Hasan." I cut my eye at him.

"My bad. We got stuff to do."

Heather didn't move, and I couldn't help but to step in for the sake of time and what little patience I had left.

"It's fine. We…"

"Nah. It's not fine, and she's not wearing this. She's wearing the dress you bought her." Focusing his attention back on Heather, he spoke. "Get the dress so she can change." Everything in his demeanor and tone told me he was not playing. She must've known it too because she made a beeline toward the back.

"C'mon, Bells. We gotta hurry up so we can take our pictures."

Heather returned just as quickly as she left, this time with the dress in the same shopping bag it was in when I bought it and a pair of shoe boots.

"Childish as hell, man," Hasan let out, taking the bag from her. Swapping the pageant dress for the new one, he looked over at me. "She straight?"

"Yeah."

"Aight. Where's her coat?"

"Right here." She handed him a fur coat with a pair of gloves and a hat. "What time you think you'll be back, so I can let my sister know?"

"We'll be back sometime tomorrow." Swooping Bella up in his arms, he took my hand, and we walked out of the door.

This was the Hasan I'd come to know. He didn't give a fuck, and when it came down to me, he was going to make sure I was good around whoever, whenever.

I TAPPED my fingers anxiously on the window ledge of the car while my eyes flickered between the clock on the dashboard and the slow moving traffic ahead. We'd taken a wrong turn, adding another fifteen minutes to our drive, which made me less than hopeful about making it to the studio in time. Shifting in my seat, frustration began to settle in.

"We're gonna be late. I wanted this to be perfect. Showing up late to the place is not my idea of perfection."

Hasan reached over and placed his hand on my stomach. "Chill out before you stress my baby and there won't be a photoshoot. We're almost there, and them people gon' wait. Even if I have to pay extra, we're getting the shoot done today, but you gotta relax."

"Okay." Placing my hand atop of his, the baby kicked, alerting us to their presence.

"I know, baby. Daddy told her."

"Don't be trying to use the baby to gang up on me, especially when my partner back there locked in with *Gracie's Corner*."

He glanced back, and we both laughed. Bella could care less about anything that was going on when Gracie was on the screen.

"You're definitely on your own, Ma."

"Exactly."

"We're almost there though. Look, the GPS says five minutes." He pointed to the screen on the dashboard, and I nodded.

As the traffic began to thin, he expertly navigated the car through our exit. I only hoped that the people at the studio were both courteous and understanding of our tardiness. I wasn't above pulling the pregnancy card. I always had a Braxton Hicks contraction excuse on standby. Pulling onto the street of the address, my phone vibrated in the cupholder. Picking it up, there was a text notification from my cousin that read, "I can't wait to see you, boo!"

Confused, I unlocked the phone to call my mother. The phone rang once before she answered.

"Hey, Big Mama."

"Dang, were you waiting by the phone for me to call?" I joked.

"Girl, I've been having my phone practically glued to my hand ever since you told me you were pregnant. I gotta be ready for when my grandbaby makes her debut. Wassup? You having contractions?"

Giggling, I replied. **"No, ma'am. We're still baking."**

Since finding out about her grandchild, my mother had been at my beck and call. She checked on me twice a day, and whenever I didn't feel like doing something, she was right there if Hasan, Brae'lynn, or Asani weren't available, and that was a rarity. She and Hasan had a schedule and took turns making sure that Big Mama was well taken care of.

"Okay. What you need? I'm in the middle of decorating my tree."

"Awww, Ma. You were supposed to wait for me."

"So you can be over here doing the most then I gotta hear Hasan's mouth? No, ma'am. I got this."

"Well, whose gonna put the star at the top? I always do it."

"Me, girl. I'm gonna use the step ladder."

"Be careful, Ma."

"I will. But what you call for if it's not about my gran?"

"Oh, Tia sent me a message saying she couldn't wait to see me. Are you hosting Christmas brunch at the restaurant this year, and I don't know about it?"

Before my father passed, Christmas had been our family's holiday. We hosted a brunch at the bakery for the family that was a hit every year. We'd exchange gifts, and all of the kids would put on a talent show for the adults. After losing my dad, my mother didn't feel right hosting the brunch without him, so she put a pause on the celebration. Everyone understood and respected her decision.

"Yeah. I thought I told you."

"Ummm, no. I don't think you did. Then again, this pregnancy brain can get to me sometimes. I'm excited to hear that though. What you need me to do?"

"Nothing," she and Hasan said at the same time. She laughed while he winked at me.

"Thank you, son," she said loud enough for him to hear. **"All I need you to do is show up. And if my gran comes before then, stay the hell home."**

"But..."

"But my ass. You heard what I said, Riz."

Sucking my teeth, I conceded. **"Alright, I gotta go. We just pulled up to the studio for the photoshoot."**

"Okay. I love you. Have fun."

"I love you too, Mommy." Ending the call, I tossed my phone in my purse. "You want me to get Bells?"

"Nah. I got that baby. You handle the one in there." He pointed to my belly.

As we approached the studio entrance, a sense of anticipation came over me, prompting me to glance over my shoulder at Hasan, who was trailing behind me with Bella.

"What happened?" he questioned with a raised brow.

"Nothing." I continued forward.

Reaching around me, he opened the door. I followed the directions of the booking site, entering and walking down a quiet hallway in search of Studio B. The place was quiet — almost deliberately quiet as if the world was holding its breath for some reason. I stopped walking and turned to Hasan.

"Bae, why is it so quiet in here?"

"Shit, hell if I know. Got a nigga feeling like we being set up or some shit. You know I'm shell."

"Boy, ain't nobody settin' us up," I said, cautiously moving forward. "This is it right here. Studio B."

"Okay. Open the door," he urged.

"Open door, Risma," Bella added, and I chuckled, placing my hand on the handle.

With the sudden urge to brace myself, I took a deep breath before pushing the door open. The joyous shout of "Surprise!" made me freeze. My eyes widened in amazement as the familiar faces of our family and small circle of friends filled the studio space. In shock, I stepped forward, blinking back the emotions swelling up in me to avoid a makeup disaster.

The trail of silver and teal balloons floated toward the high ceiling, and the spacious room was tastefully decorated with pictures from our maternity shoot aligning the walls. I had the slightest clue what was going on, but as the crowd parted, my heart leaped at the white rose archway with the words WILL YOU MARRY ME in the middle of it. With shaky hands, I slowly turned to find Hasan down on one knee. My makeup didn't stand a chance against the tears that blurred my vision.

"Charisma," he began, his voice laced with emotion yet confident, "who would've known that me beating a nigga's ass would lead me to the love of my life?" Laughter echoed throughout the room, making me giggle through my tears. "You didn't have to chase me, and I didn't seek you out because God saw fit for us to be one. Outside of Bella and our little one on the way, you've become the easiest person in my life to love."

In the moment, everyone in the room faded, and silence fell around us. My heart pounded as each word he expressed weaved through me, powerful and true.

"My father always told me that my heart would choose my wife," he continued. "My heart chose you the day we were set up by our mothers. The way you've embraced Bells further lets me know without a doubt that I'm doing the right thing. With a reflection of our love growing in your womb, I want to make this forever official. Will you do me the honor and take a nigga off the market for good?"

In his hand appeared **my** engagement ring. The ring I'd shown him as **thee** ring for me. The beautiful, feminine, sleek, three-carat, Brilliant Love diamond ring from Harry Winston was stunning. Using the back of my hand to pat my tears away, I leaned over and placed my hands on his cheeks.

"You betta not get yo pregnant ass down there with him!" I heard my mother yell out from the crowd.

Chuckling, Hasan stood. "I don't want no beef."

"Yes, Hasan." I managed a whisper. "Yes, I'll take your player's card."

A collective cheer erupted as he placed the ring on my finger and kissed my lips. The make out session didn't last long before we were swarmed by the family.

"I love you," he professed.

"I love you so much."

This was a moment in time that a picture couldn't capture. It was something you had to witness in person. My heart was full, and I just knew the day couldn't get any better than this.

Hasan

As we celebrated our engagement, I watched Charisma from across the room showing off her ring to the women, and an accomplished smile spread across my face. My weeks of preparation had paid off in a big way. The fact that I was able to make it happen without her trying to figure out what was going on was nothing but pure luck. She hated to be left out of anything, so I had to play it cool. I had no idea I was going to propose until I **knew**. It felt right, so I went with that feeling.

Prior to my relationship with Charisma, marriage had never crossed my mind. I wasn't scared of the idea but hesitant about choosing the right person. Riz was it. And knowing I needed a woman's touch to give her the proposal of her dreams, I contacted the people who knew her best, her best friends and her mother. I hit Brae'lynn first, knowing she'd be instrumental in ensuring that Charisma was on point for the day. The idea to use the photoshoot as a cover up for the surprise was all her doing. We'd met up at her new juice bar where I laid out my plan.

"Brae'lynn, I need your help," I expressed, taking a seat across from her.

"I ain't got no money," she joked, sipping the fresh carrot juice she blended.

"Maann, I don't need no money." I chuckled.

"Okay, cool. Wassup? And does Riz know you're here?"

"No. I'm here about her."

"Oh, what's wrong?" She sat up straight and pushed the juice aside.

"I'm gonna propose to her."

Brae'lynn's eyes widened, and then she gave a knowing smile. "Goddamit, it's about time. What you need me and Asani to do?"

"I want it to be a surprise. She wants to book a holiday photoshoot with Bella next week. You think you can help her with that and get me all the details? I'll handle the rest."

"I'll do you one better. A friend of mine owns a studio. I'll point her in that direction and get with my homegirl to coordinate the surprise."

"That's perfect. Get me the details as soon as you can. Thanks, Brae'lynn."

"No thanks needed. My sis deserves it all. Now get outta here before I start crying."

With Brae'lynn and Asani locked in on their task, I reached out to Ms. Cheryl next. With Charisma's dad being gone, I knew that getting Ms. Cheryl's blessing would mean the world to her. We'd grown a close bond, and she'd been instrumental in the rebuilding of my relationship with my mother. I valued her opinion.

"Hey, son. What's going on?" *She greeted once the call connected.*

"Hey, Ma. You got a minute to talk?"

"Big Mama and gran okay?"

"Yep."

"Okay, what you need?"

"I want to propose to Charisma, but I can't move forward without your blessing. I wanna go to the cemetery and talk to her dad about it too."

There was a quiet pause, but I could still hear breathing on the line.

"Last night, my husband visited me in my dreams as he often does. He told me that he was ready to let his baby girl go. I didn't fully understand what he meant by that, but I do now. Hasan, you have my blessing and his too. How can I help?"

With everyone in place, I was able to give Charisma the proposal she deserved in front of the people she loved most.

"Say, nephew, I wish you would've let me in on your little secret," my uncle said, grabbing me by my shoulder. "Look at my guy, the family man. You're making me proud. Congratulations."

"Thanks, Unc. I see Liv over there amongst the women. I think she's ready for a ring of her own."

He took a sip of what I was sure was some kind of whiskey in his cup and nodded. "She'll get hers soon. Right now, it's about you and Charisma. Can I offer you one piece of advice?"

"I'm listenin'."

Standing in front of me, he trained his eyes on mine before continuing to speak. "Being engaged is a beautiful thing, but no woman wants to be a fiancée for long. You just set the tone. Don't have that woman walkin' round here wearing the title of fiancée out. You hear me?"

I nodded, taking in his advice. "I hear you."

"Cool. I gotta head out. I love you." Dapping me up, he pulled me in for a manly hug. "Keep making your old man proud. He always wanted the best for you. This is part of that plan."

I watched as he walked off and thought about my father. With the exception of my line of work, I knew my old man was smiling down on me and ordering my steps.

"Look at you, bout to be someone's husband." Turning, I found my mother standing behind me with Bella at her side.

"Daddy, up." She held her hands out to me, and I complied with her request.

"If it were up to you, this little girl's feet would never touch the ground." She smirked.

"This is a fact. Hey, Ma. You look nice." I pulled her in for a hug, and she embraced me tightly.

Every time she hugged me, it felt like she was making up for the ones she missed out on over the years. Her *I love yous* were always extra heartfelt as well.

"Thank you, son. How do you feel?"

"I feel blessed. Happy."

"I can see it all over you. The two of you exude happiness. You found your perfect person. And son, let me tell you, nothing in life feels better than that. Now, I know I'm not your dad or your uncle, but if there's any advice you need, please pick up the phone and call Mommy. I know a thing or two about what it takes to have a successful marriage."

"I definitely will." I'd already had an idea of who I'd seek counsel from should I need it. My mother was at the top of my list.

Growing up, I watched my parents and how they treated each other. My father provided the house, but it was my mother's love and care that made it a home. While he brought in the money, she managed the finances. If my father was the head of the family, she was the neck that held him up. A helpmate in every sense of the word.

"Any plans for Christmas?"

"We're trying to stay close to the home in the event Riz goes into labor at that time."

"I can just imagine how spoiled that baby will be if they're born on Christmas."

"Risma," Bells called out.

Turning, I could see Charisma making her way over to us. She had one hand on her back and one hand on her stomach. It was a sign that it was time to get Big Mama home.

"Hey, Ma." She greeted my mother with a hug. "C'mon, Bells." She reached for Bella, and I shook my head no.

"Riz can't carry you, Bells. She gotta carry your baby, remember?" I rubbed Charisma's belly for emphasis. Bella wasn't trying to hear it though.

"Come to Gran, Bells. Gran carry you." Climbing out of my arms and into my mother's, she rested her head on her chest.

"Soon, Bella Boop." Charisma assured her with a kiss on her cheek.

"Y'all a mess," my mother let out, laughing, before walking off.

Pulling Charisma to the front of me, I kissed her forehead. "Tuck your lip in. She'll be aight."

"I know. Can you kiss me?"

"Kiss the shit out you." Kissing her lips twice, I went in for a third, sucking her bottom lip into my mouth this time, pulling a moan from her. "There's a bathroom in here somewhere. You can get fucked moaning like that."

She giggled against my lips and pulled back. "I know."

"Were you surprised?"

"Very. I couldn't have imagined a proposal today. You really went all out, baby. Thank you."

"The world is yours so long as you're mine."

"If the world is mine, where these other people gon' live?" she asked with a goofy grin.

"I really don't give a damn."

Laughing, she wrapped her arms around me and placed her head on my chest. "Is the surprise over?"

"Why? You want something else?"

"Yes... our bed."

"You sleepy?"

"No. I just wanna get you in it, so I can show you just how appreciative I am for you making this the best proposal ever."

"You gon' put it in the back of your throat?"

"Uh huh."

"Copy."

As fast as the celebration started, it had to end. I wanted to see what that fiancée head was hittin' on cause that girlfriend top had a nigga head gone.

WAKING UP THE NEXT MORNING, I could smell bacon and cinnamon in the air. Seeing Charisma's side of the bed empty, I knew she was downstairs working the pots. An early bird, she always saw to it that she was up before me to ensure I had some type of food on my stomach before I left the house. Pulling the comforter off my body, I stood and headed to the bathroom to take care of my morning hygiene. Entering the bathroom, there was a yellow sticky note on the mirror with a handwritten note from her.

Before you brush your teeth and wash your face, I just thought you should know that you woke up someone's fine ass fiancé today. Oh, and that dick you laid down last night got me feeling on top of the world this morning. Carry on, King.

Laughing, I brushed my teeth and washed my face. Drying

my hands, I took the note down and headed downstairs to the kitchen.

"Okay, Bells. We can do our Christmas colors white, red, and gold, or blue, white, and silver. Which one you like?" Charisma held two packs of ornaments up for Bella who could care less about the colors so long as they were shiny and on a tree.

"Blue, white, and silver," I answered for her. "Good morning, Daddy's girls." Swooping Bella up from the kitchen island, I kissed her cheek and leaned over to kiss Charisma's lips. "How she get up here?"

"Huh?" Riz questioned as if she didn't hear me.

"You heard me. Stop picking her up. I'm serious."

"Alrighttt," she dragged.

"Keep it up and I'ma tell ya mom."

"That's so childish. But you got it. You eating?"

"Yep."

"Okay. I'll make your plate. We ate already."

"You sit down. I'll make my plate."

Without fuss, she took a seat and let me move about the kitchen. Placing Bella in her highchair, I piled my plate with grits, sausage, and eggs. Pouring myself a glass of apple juice, I sat down next to her.

"You have any plans today?" she asked, resting her head on my shoulder.

"Nah. Why? You wanna do something?"

"I wanna put the tree up in Bella's room and put together the rest of the baby's furniture."

"We can do that. We meaning **I** can put the furniture together while you and Bella watch." I had to be clear on the assignment for little Ms. Iwannadoeverything.

"Can I at least hang pictures on the walls? It doesn't require much effort. Quick nail in the wall, picture up." Holding her hand out, she demonstrated the process she had described.

"Aight," I agreed, chewing a piece of bacon.

After breakfast, she cleaned the dishes while I took Bella upstairs to get her settled. Figuring it would be best to set up the baby furniture first, I set Bella up in the baby's room. Pulling each box from the closet, I set the pictures along the wall for Charisma and got started on putting together the furniture.

Minutes later, she appeared in the doorway with a tape measurer and a small hammer. "Need help?"

"I got this part," I assured her. "You work on hanging those pictures, Mrs. Fix It."

With a playful salute, she began arranging the frames and tools she needed for set up. As I organized the pieces to the crib, I glanced over and watched her meticulously measure the height for the first photo. Her attention to detail was one of the things I loved about her.

"This look crooked, bae?" she questioned, holding a framed picture of a 3D sonogram of our baby's face up against the wall.

"No. You good."

"Okay."

We spent the next few hours assembling furniture, hanging pictures, and organizing. By the time I got around to putting up Bella's tree, both she and Charisma had left me to take a nap. Leaving the star for Bells to put up, I retired back to my bedroom and climbed in bed behind Charisma. Feeling my presence, she scooted back and laid in the crook of my arm.

"Everything put up?" she asked through a yawn.

"Yeah. Daddy took care of it." I kissed the back of her neck.

"Thank you, Daddy."

"The sticky note was a nice touch this morning."

"And I'm your fine ass fiancée, so it's a win-win."

"That it is."

Feeling accomplished, I drifted off to sleep.

Charisma

Pushing my cart through the aisles of Whole Foods, I bobbed my head to the Christmas music. The supermarket was the last place I should've been considering I'd told Hasan that I would stay off my feet after complaining about back pain over the last few days. But when those pregnancy cravings hit, I had to have what I wanted as soon as the thought entered my mind. Tonight, it was butter pecan ice cream, sunflower seeds, and cheddar cheese Pringles.

Picking up my last item, I made my way up to the register. Just as I thought I'd gotten away with sneaking out, Sza's *Snooze* played from my phone. Bracing myself for Hasan's loving wrath, I answered the call.

"You leaving the house with my baby without telling me now?" he questioned in a disapproving tone.

Knowing he had my location, I didn't attempt to lie. **"I wanted some ice cream, baby. I'm checking out now."**

"I ain't get no messages bout no ice cream."

"You're out handling business. I don't wanna keep calling every time I need something."

"Do I work a nine to five?"

"No."

"Exactly. I don't punch a clock, so I move how I wanna move. You can go into labor at any time. Not letting me know what you got going on at all times don't sit well with me. If you need something, you call. This shit take a backseat to you and my seed. Stop being hardheaded."

"Okay. It won't happen again." Unloading my cart, I placed my items on the conveyor belt, and a sharp pain hit my pelvis, making me lean over and grab hold of the register. **"Oouu, sssss,"** I let out through gritted teeth. Closing my eyes, I rocked back-and-forth.

"Ma'am, are you okay?" the cashier asked with concerned eyes.

"Bae?" Hasan called out to me.

Taking a shallow and slow breath, I nodded, giving the cashier a reassuring smile. **"I'm okay, baby. Just a little sore-ness. But I'm good.** You can go head and scan, ma'am." I let the cashier know, hoping that my tone didn't convey the instant worry that surged through my body.

It was clear that my face told it all because the cashier had yet to move even though there was a line forming behind me.

"Girl, I'm okay," I said with light humor that clearly wasn't conveyed through the phone to Hasan.

I could hear his breathing quicken on the other end of the phone before his concern worked its way through our connection.

"Charisma, are you in pain?"

"I'm alright, Hasan. It was just one of those random pains. Your baby in there clubbin'. I'm checking out now."

He sighed deeply, a clear indication that he didn't believe a word I said. Scanning my items, the cashier gave me a sympathetic smile as I swiped my debit card to pay. Packing my groceries, she handed me the bag and my receipt.

"You take it easy, okay? Looks like it can be any day now."

A polite smile appeared on my face, but in my head, I was cussin' her out. She didn't need to say all that with this man on the phone.

"I will. Thanks." Walking as fast as my belly and the familiar pain in my back would allow me, I made my way to the car.

"Baby, you still there?"

"Yeah, I'm here. You good to drive?"

"Yes."

"You got a hat on?"

"Hasan." I stopped short of my car.

"What? You leaving out the house without letting me know where you are. I wouldn't put it past you to be out there without a hat."

"I have it on, smart ass. A scarf too."

"Uh, huh. I'm close to the house. Come straight here," he commanded.

Juggling my cravings in one hand and my phone in the other, I made it to the car. Sliding into the driver's side, I sat the snacks on the passenger seat and started the car. Connecting my phone to the Bluetooth, I adjusted my seat at an angle suitable to my aching back.

"I'm coming, sir."

"Straight here, Charisma. Don't pass go, don't collect $200."

"Okay, baby. Can I hang up, so I can listen to my music?"

"Yeah. I love you."

"I love you more."

Ending the call with the worrywart, I pulled slowly out of the parking lot and onto the expressway, hoping that the sharp pain was just an extra nudge from the baby and nothing serious. Rubbing my stomach, I spoke out loud. "Hold tight, boo. You got a couple more days to bake."

I pulled into the driveway and could barely put the car in park before Hasan was outside and walking over to me. Rolling down my window, I stuck my head out with my lips puckered for him to kiss. Never one to deny me, he pressed his lips against mine twice.

"See? Home safe and sound. Me and my snacks. You mad at me?"

"No. I'm not mad. And I don't want you to think that I'm

tryna keep you locked up in the crib either. I just don't like seeing you in pain, bae."

"I know. I'ma sit down forreal."

He smirked. "That's cap. But I'd appreciate it if you just made the effort."

Grinning, I replied. "I can do that."

"I'ma hold you to it. Come on, let's get inside. It's cold as hell out here."

Grabbing my purse and the grocery bag, I stepped out of the car. As both of my feet touched the ground, the sharp pain hit me again. He picked up on it immediately.

"Contraction?"

I nodded in confirmation. "I think it's really happening this time. Sssss, owww." I held his hand and squeezed his shoulder.

That was all he needed as he pulled out his phone to contact my doctor. His tone was steady, and I could tell he was trying to keep calm to avoid me coming undone. I felt another pain, this one stronger than the other, causing me to bury my face in his neck.

"Yeah. They're definitely contractions." I heard him say. "It won't take us long to get to the hospital. We'll see you there."

"Ooouu, shit, bae. These are contraction contractions. What the doctor say?"

"Come straight to the hospital and they'll take us straight up to labor and delivery. Come on, we'll take this car." Slowly escorting me over to the passenger side, he helped me in and ran back over to the driver's side.

Looking over at my ice cream, I shook my head.

"We'll get you another one," he assured me, reading my mind.

"Thank you, baby. You're so... Ahhhh!" I yelped.

"Breathe, baby," he coached, manning the wheel with one hand and rubbing my stomach with the other. "Breathe."

The drive to the hospital was a blur of contractions and deep breaths mixed with Hasan's reassuring words of everything being alright. While I believed that, the reality that I might really be in labor scared me a little. There was no amount of preparation that could've prepared me for the moment. It felt like everything we had planned went out the window in an instant. Finally arriving at the hospital, the bright lights of the emergency and medical staff all around were both comforting and overwhelming. It was comforting in the sense that I knew if our baby decided to make its debut now, the medical staff was close, but overwhelming in knowing that there was a high chance that it would happen. Before I knew it, I was in a room with my legs cocked open and my doctor checking my cervix.

"So, wassup, Dr. Clarke? Are we having a baby today?"

"Not today, Mommy and Daddy," she confirmed, rolling back in the small stool she sat on and pulling off her gloves. "You're about two centimeters dilated though. Have you been staying off your feet?"

Hasan looked down at me from where he stood at the side of my bed. He wasn't gonna put me out there, but his eyes urged me to tell the truth.

"I have for the most part, but I could do better."

"I need you to do your absolute best. I have a feeling that

we'll be back here soon. And it won't be for a warmup. It'll be the real thing." Standing from the stool, she discarded her gloves in the garbage and headed for the door. "If anything changes, be sure to call me. And if you can't get me, come straight here."

"Okay. Oh, wait. Since we're getting closer to the due date, I think I wanna give Hasan one of his Christmas gifts now. Can you tell him the sex of the baby?"

Hasan grinned and nodded. "Go head and tell me what I already know, Dr. Clarke."

Smiling, she replied. "Get ready for a lot of bows and barrettes. You're having a little princess."

Leaving the room, she left me with a beaming Hasan.

"You happy?"

"Happy as hell." Leaning down, he kissed my lips, then my cheeks, and my forehead. "She just confirmed what I already knew."

"Can we tell everyone at the Christmas brunch?"

"Whatever you wanna do, baby."

"Okay. Let's get outta here so we can go get me some new ice cream."

"Come on, Big Mama."

Helping me into my pants and shoes, we left the labor and delivery unit and headed to the car. I had an extra pep in my step on the way there just thinking about the trinity of snacks that awaited me. After today, I had every intention on sitting down like the doctor suggested. And I could bet that Hasan would be right next to me, making sure that I did.

THE DRIVE HOME after the false labor and delivery was a relaxed one. Hasan had stopped to pick up my pint of butter pecan ice cream as promised, and all was right with the world.

"I think we should go over that list of names we came up with when we get home," he suggested. "There's a few we can cross out off rip."

"Which ones? And you better not say Ocean."

"Damn, bae. You fine and psychic? That shit is wild."

Laughing, I hit his arm. "Shut up. You said we could leave the name on the list as a possibility. Remember, you said to write the name in the middle of the paper because you were on the fence."

"Did you give me some pussy before we went over the names?"

I didn't have to think about my answer seeing as he'd been doing me nasty every other night faithfully. "Yes."

"Well, then, anything I said after that can't be used against me. A nigga mind be gone after I go swimming." Reaching over, he squeezed my thigh.

"You aggravating," I said, my panties moist at his touch.

As we turned onto our street, his phone buzzed in the cupholder. Picking it up, he gave it a quick glance and sighed before turning it to me. There was an incoming call from Heather on the screen. Knowing that her call could possibly have something to do with Bella, I nodded for him to answer.

"Wassup, Heather?"

"Hey, Hasan. It's Jamie. I'm calling from Heather's phone because Bella got into an accident at my house." The voice on the other end went silent and so did Hasan for a few seconds.

"What happened, and where my baby?" He gripped the steering wheel tightly, and his jaw flexed. I reached out to rub his arm, hoping it would be soothing enough to calm him.

"She was playing with the boys and fell off the top bunk of their bunk bed. We're at the hospital."

"You mean to fuckin' tell me that y'all jus now getting around to calling her father after going to the hospital? What typa bullshit is that, Jamie?!" he snapped, and I felt the car shift as he made a sharp turn.

"I... she..."

"Just tell me which hospital, Jamie."

"Presbyterian," she responded quickly. **"The one near my house. And..."**

He ended the call, and the car lurched forward.

"Bae!" I yelled out, alerting him to my very pregnant presence. "Baby on board."

"Damn. I'm sorry, baby."

"It's okay. Pull over so I can drive." The last thing we needed was to get pulled over or even worse, a car accident.

"I got it." His eyes didn't leave the road as he spoke. "You got your seatbelt on?"

"Yes, but you have to slow down, Hasan." I kept my voice calm to avoid heightening an already sensitive situation.

"I gotta get to my Bells." He pulled back on the gas a little, easing my nervousness.

Reaching over, I rubbed the back of his neck as I'd seen my mother do to my father when he was stressed.

"We're gonna get there, baby. And Bella is gonna be good. Our girl is tough."

"I know, but how they let my baby fall off a fucking bunk bed?! I keep tellin' Heather every time she goes over there to keep Bella close cause them bad ass kids her sister got don't care about life. These lil' niggas only five and six and be doing the craziest shit."

I wanted to say kids would be kids, but I didn't know the full scope of the situation nor the kids involved. So, I simply reiterated that she was going to be fine while praying that was the case once we got there.

Hasan

I held Bella in my lap with her iPad propped up to keep her preoccupied while the doctor wrapped her wrist and gave instructions on her aftercare. Heather stood back, away from me but close enough to keep watch. I hadn't said more than two words to her since I'd entered the hospital room. She knew I was tight, and there was nothing she could say to make the situation right. I'd promised Charisma that I wouldn't click out when I saw Heather, but the longer I was in her presence, the more irritated I became.

Charisma opted to sit in the waiting room as to not crowd Bella, but I knew better. She was trying to avoid confrontation. And while I appreciated that, I didn't want Heather to feel like she was running my woman off. The doctor wrapped the final layer on Bella's wrist, and when she went to pin it, Bella broke out in a wail.

"Oh, sweetie, I'm sorry," the doctor spoke empathetically. "We're all set. I promise."

Heather walked over to console her. "It's okay, baby."

"You did great, Bella. Are there any questions or concerns about her aftercare? Anything I need to go over again?"

"No," Heather answered. "We got it."

"Great. Like I mentioned, she can take the over-the-counter Tylenol for the pain or any discomfort."

"Thanks for taking care of her," I said.

"Oh, she was a joy and a tough cookie, might I add. The nurse will be back in shortly with your discharge paperwork. Be sure to follow up with her pediatrician in the next day or so. And no more flying off those bunk beds, okay, Supergirl? Here you go." She handed Bella a lollipop to which she accepted with a smile. "Have a good day."

"I'ma take her home with me. I'll pick up the Tylenol on my way," I let Heather know as the doctor exited the room. She just stared at me without a response. "What?"

"Nothing." She rolled her big ass eyes and sucked her teeth. "You know you didn't have to hang up on my sister like that. She only called because I was tending to Bella. And you could've told me that you were coming with Charisma."

"What you wanted me to do, stay on the phone and kick it with your sister? There wasn't shit else to talk about after hearing my baby was hurt. You, as the parent, should've called on the way to the hospital. And don't worry bout where my woman go. Anywhere I'm at, she will be if I deem it necessary."

"Okay, but you doing that makes it seem like you feel a way

toward her. What happened was an accident. Jamie already feels bad enough."

"I ain't making it seem like shit. I do feel a way. My daughter got hurt because she wasn't being properly supervised. I don't know any three-year-olds just jumping off bunk beds and shit willingly. Your sister need to get a hold on her boys or get some help. Better yet, point me in the direction of they bum ass father, so I can whip that nigga ass for not doing his part."

"All that cussing you doing in front of her is really unnecessary."

I usually didn't cuss as much in front of Bella, but I was pissed off, and the fact that she wasn't seeing my point was making it worse.

"Daddy, broke." Bella pointed to the black screen on the iPad. Standing up with her in my arms, I tucked it under my arm.

"It's not broken, baby. It died. Daddy gotta charge it for you when we get home."

"It was an accident, Hasan. Kids play. and sometimes they're too rough. We both got after the boys." Her explanation in defense of her sister went in one ear and out the other.

"Our **daughter** is three." I put emphasis on the fact that she was a girl. "All that *kids will be kids* shit don't apply to a three-year-old, not mine anyway. And you tryna use that logic to justify what happened is about to blow me, so let's stop talkin' bout it. Where's her coat and stuff?"

Snatching Bella's things up off the bed, she handed it to me. Unfazed by her attitude, I put Bella's headband and coat on, careful not to disrupt her injury. I could see Heather clenching her jaw and her eyes narrowing slightly. She wanted to say more, but before she could come up with a rebuttal, the nurse returned with the discharge papers and instructions.

"Alright, Ms. Bella, all good to go?" The extra chirp in the nurse's voice seemed to irritate Heather, making her already narrow eyes turn into slits.

Bella nodded bravely with her lollipop clasped tightly in her good hand.

Thanking the nurse, I left out and headed for the waiting room to find Charisma with Heather lagging behind me. Sensing my presence, Charisma turned and stood up. Stretching uncomfortably, she made her way over to us.

"Hey, Bells," she greeted softly, her face filled with love and concern. "You got a boo boo?"

"Hurt me, Risma," Bella mumbled in her small voice, resting her head on my shoulder.

"I see. We gonna fix it though. Right, Daddy?" She looked to me, and I nodded.

"We're taking her home," I announced before turning Bella to Heather to say her goodbyes.

"Mommy love you. Please call me if anything changes with her. I really think she should come home with me. Y'all got enough to deal with."

"She's not an extra," Charisma spoke up. "She's a part of the household. We'll manage."

With a brief but civil smile, Heather kissed Bella's cheek and went on her way. Fluffing the puff on Bella's hair, Charisma shot me a glance.

"What?"

"Nothing," I replied. "You handled that well. I been waiting on you."

She smirked. "What Kendrick say? Sometimes you gotta pop out and show niggas."

Chuckling, I put my arm around her waist. "Exactly. Let's go. I done seen enough hospitals for the day." We walked hand in hand out of the hospital, looking like the picture-perfect family. I fully understood why Heather felt the way she did.

FINALLY ARRIVING HOME after a stop to Rite Aid, Charisma hopped out first and headed inside to start on dinner. After the eventful day we had, I suggested that we pick something up, but she insisted on making Bella's favorite meal instead. So, baked ziti and cheesy garlic bread it was. I carried Bella inside, kissing the top of her forehead, hoping my presence comforted her. On the ride home, she tried to break down her fall as best as her three-year-old mind could with me and Charisma hanging onto her every word.

"Alright, Supergirl, Daddy gonna get you changed, and we're gonna chill while Riz makes dinner. You hungry?"

She nodded drowsily. "My iPad."

"Okay. Lemme charge it and I'll set it up after you change."

Setting her down on the living room couch, I plugged the

iPad into an available outlet and headed to her room to grab a pair of pajamas. As I sifted through her drawers, my phone rang in my pocket. Checking to see who was calling, I wasn't surprised to see Heather's name on my caller id. I wanted to ignore it, but with Bella's condition, I didn't want to keep her from knowing what was going on as she'd done me.

"Wassup?"

"Just calling to see if you stopped at the store to get the Tylenol."

"Yeah. We got it. I'm about to give her the first dose once I change her clothes."

"Okay," she replied and went silent for a few seconds.

"Aight. I'll keep you posted." All I had was an update for her. I wasn't interested in any other conversation.

"Wait, Hasan. I need to say something."

Sighing, I waited for her to continue.

"You there?"

"Yeah. Go head."

"Look, I'm not trying to beef witchu. Our coparenting relationship has never been difficult, and I don't want that for Bella."

"Okay."

"Okay? That's it?"

"Yeah. I've never had an issue communicating with you until now, and that's because you made it an issue. Let's be real, the only thing that has changed is the fact that I have someone permanent in my life now. It hasn't taken away from me being a father. In fact, having

Charisma has added to the list of people who love our daughter."

"You're right. And for the sake of Bella, I'm making this call. And for the holidays." She laughed lightly.

"Okay. Well, this is a start. Have a goodnight."

"You too. And kiss Bells for me."

Ending the call, I walked back into the living room where Bells and Charisma lay snuggled up. Standing silently in the doorway, I listened as the two talked to the new baby, letting her know what all she had to look forward to once she came home. Bella's small hand rested on Charisma's stomach, her face a picture of innocence and fascination.

"We gotta come up with a name for her, Bells. You wanna help me and Daddy pick out a name?"

"Her name, Risma."

Charisma giggled. "Yeah. We gotta give her a pretty name like yours."

My heart swelled with pride at their exchange. Their bond had developed naturally to a point where there were times when she'd choose Charisma over me. As soon as her belly began to grow, Bella was attached to her hip. Seeing her so eager and loving about the sibling she had yet to meet made me feel even better about our growing family. Walking over to join them, I sat down on the couch and placed Charisma's legs on my lap.

"Y'all look comfortable."

"We are. We're talking to our baby."

"I just got off the phone with Heather. She's waving the white flag."

"Oh, yeah? How so?"

"Basically, she wants to do better with communication and get our coparenting back to where it was, I guess."

"I'm happy that y'all came to that consensus. Although Bella is only three and too young to understand the dynamic between you two, it's good that she sees positive interaction between her parents. I know my presence sickens baby mama number one, but y'all being in a good space helps me too."

"How?" I questioned with a raised brow.

She sat up and put her hands over Bella's ears. "It keeps me from having to tap that ass when she pisses you off." Her eyes sparkled with mischief, making me laugh.

"Type shit." I held out my fist for her to dap, gesturing our partnership and mutual understanding that it was us against everybody.

The brief exchange showed Charisma's unwavering support of ultimately wanting the best for me and Bells, despite the situation. And there was a sense of peace and certainty in knowing that my woman always had the best interest for our family as a whole at the forefront of her mind.

Charisma

As the first flakes of winter had began to fall outside, giving way to the official sign of Christmas, I was nestled comfortably on the couch with a warm throw blanket covering my body. I'd awakened to a note from Hasan that he and Bells would be gone most of the day Christmas shopping and would check on me periodically. He made sure to remind me of Dr. Clarke's suggestion and his orders to stay off my feet as much as possible. I sighed at the note but nodded my understanding as if he were around to see it. The whole staying put thing felt constraining at times, but I knew it was all for the health of our baby, so I complied.

Just as I was settling in to watch the Christmas episode of *Martin*, the doorbell rang. I wasn't expecting anyone or anything, but when I heard the familiar impatient knock, followed by my name being called, a smile crept on my face. My besties were here which only meant that Hasan had planned their visit to surprise me. He knew I hated to be alone for extended periods of time, and with him having taken Bella on the shopping trip, I appreciated the company.

"I'm comingggg!" I yelled out in a song like tone, unwrapping myself from the blanket and pushing up from the couch.

Making it to the door, I opened it, and the girls rushed in with bags in their hands and flushed faces from the cold air.

"Listen, I'ma need you to either leave the door unlocked or give us a key. It's too damn cold to be standing out there waiting for you to get to the door," Brae'lynn complained as I closed the door behind them. "And I gotta pee."

I chuckled. "I was moving as fast as I can, heffa. And you always gotta pee. You better check for a UTI."

"Shut up. Hi, Auntie baby." She rubbed my stomach. "I'll be right back to love on you after I use the bathroom."

I shook my head as she dropped the bags and scurried off to the back of the house. Turning my attention to Asani, who balanced a tray of drinks in one hand and bags in the other, I went to offer my assistance only for her to hold out the tray to me with a wide grin painted on her face.

"Hasan gave us the memo before we got here. No heavy lifting and for you not to overdo it. Here you go and thank you."

I sucked my teeth playfully and grabbed the tray. "I couldn't even sneak and do anything if I wanted to."

"No, you cannot." She kissed my cheek, and we headed for the kitchen. "How you feeling, Big Mama?"

"I'm doing good. Happy to see y'all. Please tell me one of these cups has hot chocolate in it." I eyed the three Venti sized cups from Starbucks.

"Yes. The one in the middle."

With much excitement, I grabbed my cup and took the lid off. The smell of the chocolate and peppermint was everything. "Thank youuuu."

"And I got you the pumpkin cream cheese muffin you love so much." She pulled the muffin, that looked like it was still warm, out of the bag and handed it to me.

"Awww, don't make me cry, Sani."

"Please don't," Brae'lynn interrupted as she entered the kitchen. "I'm just playing." She smiled. "Auntie babyyy." Walking around the kitchen island, she squatted in front of me and wrapped her arms around my stomach. "Can you hurry up? We're ready for you to come."

"Apparently, she's ready too. The way she's been in there C walking on my bladder is crazy."

"Wait, we're having a girl?" Asani let out hopefully.

I nodded, and they broke out in celebratory dances.

"We knew it!" Brae'lynn shouted. "I mean, we would've loved our baby either way but a girl. Oh, my God, yesssss!"

"I know. I'm excited too. Hasan is as well."

"That's a good man, Savannah."

"He really is," Asani echoed Brae'lynn's statement. "He sent a group text earlier this morning, letting us know that you could use some girl therapy. And we're here to make sure you're pampered and stress free. So, here we are with our own version of a baby moon that includes food, alcohol free libations, belly casting, and trips down memory lane."

"Awww, really? I swear I love that man so bad." I gushed over Hasan's forward thinking. He just always knew what to do and what to say.

"And to think yo' ass was so scared to tell the man that you were pregnant with his child. He won't even let yo ass sneeze without having a tissue there to wipe your nose."

I cracked up at her assessment of my baby and thought about how right she was about me being scared to death when I found out I was pregnant.

"Shit, shit, shit!" I yelled out to myself as I looked down at the three pregnancy tests on my bathroom sink that all clearly indicated that I was in fact pregnant. "What the hell, Charisma?!" I picked one of the tests up and held it up to the light as if I was checking a fake bill. Surely that was going to change the outcome of what I had read, right?

Soft knocks made me whip my head in the direction of the bathroom door. "Riz," Asani called out. "You alright?"

"Yeah, what's going on?" Brae'lynn inquired loudly. "It don't take that long to pee on a stick."

"Shut up, Brae'lynn. Damn," Sani scolded lightly.

"What? I'm tryna figure out if we gon' be aunties or not."

They spoke in whispers back-and-forth, stopping once I pulled the door open.

"It's positive. All three tests."

"Really?" they both said at the same time.

I nodded solemnly, pushing past them, and headed to the

living room. Plopping down on the couch, I buried my face in my hands.

"Why you actin' like it's the end of the world, sis? A baby is a blessing," Brae'lynn stated as if the news was just this wonderful thing.

"Brae'lynn, I barely know him. And who's to say that this is news he even wants to hear?"

"You might as well tell him, Charisma. You can't just say nothing."

"I just found out my damn self, Brae'lynn. Can I take this shit in?"

"You wanna take another one just to be sure?"

"Asani, don't do that. She done took three already. The shit say positive."

"Ughhh, y'all just don't say nothing for a minute. Let me think."

A whirlwind of emotions engulfed me, but fear and uncertainty were at the forefront. Yes, I had to tell Hasan. It was the how and when that was fucking me up.

"Let's get started with the belly cast first. We gotta commemorate the bump before baby girl comes." Asani's voice brought me back to the cheerful moment.

"Okay. Let me just text my man real quick."

"Here she go."

"Hush, hater." I slapped Brae'lynn's butt as I walked past and into the living room to my phone.

Before I could unlock it, there was a message from Hasan already waiting for me.

MYHEART: Just checking in on you. Bells got me off track, and we ended up in a toy store or three. I might be home a little later than I thought. Not too late tho. I love you, and I hope the baby moon is going well. Whatever that is.

Me: Lol. She gon' get you every time. And thank you for sending the girls over, baby. I love you.

MYHEART: Always🤍

Setting my phone back down, I removed my pajama shirt. "Let the casting begin."

~

"Nah, we really did the damn thing," Brae'lynn marveled as she and Asani carefully peeled the hardened plaster off my belly.

I was in awe at how the cast had come out. I'd seen it done on videos, but mine had come out better than I expected. It was another moment in time that I would cherish with my girls.

"Can y'all believe I'm having a baby? Like, we're really casting **my** belly."

Both Brae'lynn and Asani looked at each other before bursting out laughing.

"Girl, yes. We can believe it," Asani said. "We always knew you'd be the first to have a baby and the first one married."

"I'd be next in line, and Sani would be the very last," Brae'-lynn added.

"Hol' up now. Why would I be the last one?"

"Ion know, Sani." Brae'lynn shrugged. "Sometimes you be

giving off the vibe like niggas ain't yo cup of tea. Like you up to bat for the other team."

I snickered because there was nothing but truth in Brae'-lynn's statement. Her delivery was just extra, something we'd become accustomed to.

"You get on my nerves." Asani shoved her. "I like men, love them actually. Just not as much as you." She stuck her tongue out. "Right now, I'm getting to the bag. Love will find me."

"That's right, Sani. Just like it found me." I held up my hand, and she slapped me five. "Now, I'ma bout to be some-one's wife."

"Period!"

The day went on with us reminiscing on our college days, the trips we took as single women, and endless brunch dates where we discussed our bright futures, each memory a thread in the tapestry of our friendship.

"Oh, we got something for you. It's in your purse, Brae'lynn."

Brae'lynn lifted her head up from where she lay across the couch. While me and Asani had drank virgin piña coladas, she'd opted to spike hers.

"You gotta grab it, Sani. Between those piña coladas and the food, I can't move."

"You're such a lush," I teased.

Sani got up to get her purse and returned with a small box. "Here you go, boo."

I opened the box to find a diamond charm bracelet filled with different charms. Each charm represented a moment in our friendship. A pen for our study sessions, a Starbucks cup for our love of peppermint hot chocolates, and a baby bottle for the new chapter of life I was stepping into. I couldn't fight back the tears.

"This is so thoughtful. Thank you." I sniffled. "I don't think y'all know how much our friendship means to me. I value y'all so much, and while I'm entering what will be my new life, know that it won't change the dynamic of our friendship. I love y'all."

"Awww, we love you too, sis," Asani said through tears of her own.

Rolling off the couch, Brae'lynn made her way over to us, and we embraced each other in a tight hug.

"Since we love each other so much, I wanna let you know that expensive ass bracelet is your Christmas gift from me. I'm broke, baby."

"Bitch, get off me." I laughed. "You irritating."

"No, seriously though." She changed her tone. "We love you, and I think I speak for us both when I say we know you're gonna be an incredible mom and wife. Seeing you glow just reconfirms what we've always seen in you."

"Yeah, what she said." Asani nodded in agreement.

"And if you think this was fun, wait until the ba..." Brae'-lynn was cut off by a sharp look from Asani.

"Wait until what?"

"Until the baby comes," Asani said. "We gonna celebrate her in a big way."

"Uh huh," I replied knowingly.

They were up to something, but I would let them have it without pressing them for details. Yawning, I rubbed my belly.

"That's our cue. Come and lock up." Brae'lynn pecked my belly and stood to put on her coat.

"Thank y'all for cleaning up too. Gives Hasan one less thing to do when he gets home."

"No problem. Make sure you call or text if you need anything. No matter the time." Asani hugged me and kissed my cheek.

"I will." I waddled over to the door with them at the same time it opened.

Hasan entered with a sleeping Bella in his arms and a case of water.

"Wassup, y'all?"

"Hey, Hasan," they both spoke. Saying their goodnights to Bella, they left out.

Sitting the water down, he kissed my lips. "Hey, beautiful."

"Hi, baby. How was shopping?"

"Long and a reminder of why I hate doing it. Let me go put her down and I'll meet you in the living room where you can tell me about your day."

Settling back onto the couch, fatigue began to kick in, but I fought the urge to fall asleep because I wanted some time with my man. Returning to the living room moments later, he sat down next to me.

"Today was amazing. You keep doing things to make me fall more in love with you. You tryna outdo me on this love thing?" I asked through squinted eyes.

He chuckled. "No, baby. I'm just showing you that it's only gonna get better as time goes on. I see everything, I hear everything, and I just store it. It's how I'm able to meet a need without you even bringing it to my attention. The way you love me and show up for us and ours enables me to do that without fail. That and the way you grip a nigga up when I'm inside you." He smiled devilishly, and my clit jumped.

"I'm a little tired, but I think I have enough energy to do that lil' grip thing you like."

"Can I taste you first? I've been having a taste for something all day. And when we ate at the mall earlier, it didn't do it for me. I needed to taste you."

Biting my bottom lip, I cracked a sheepish grin while spreading my legs as I lay back on the couch. "I wouldn't dare let my fiancé go to bed hungry."

With no further words, he pulled my shorts off, exposing my wet pussy that he kept nicely trimmed during the pregnancy.

"She so pretty," he complimented, sliding two fingers up and down my slit.

"Sssssss, mmhmmm." My hips thrust upward.

"I hear you, Mama." Lifting my waist off the couch to where it was comfortable for both my back and belly, he sucked my clit into his mouth.

"Ahhhhhh, yessssss," I moaned.

Feeling his tongue inside my wet box, I creamed instantly. It didn't take much to get me there these days. Pulling his tongue out, he slid it over my clit, making it swell before sucking it into his mouth gently. My moans only made him apply more pressure followed by two fingers, this time slipping them inside of me.

"Cum for Daddy, 2A. Lemme see something."

My legs shook, and I released in his mouth again, pulling a nasty moan from him. Sitting up, he admired his handiwork.

"Pussy just glistenin'. You got this dick hard as fuck too."

Unbuckling his pants, he let them fall down to his ankles. Taking it as a sign to climb on top, I did just that. Since my belly had grown, he hadn't let me ride, so I took advantage of the moment.

"Take your time, bae. If at any moment you feel uncomfortable, we can... Shiidddd."

I slid down slowly on his shaft, not wanting to hear anything else but the sounds of our love making. Wrapping my arms around his neck, careful of my bump, I rode him slowly. In this position, I felt everything. I loved to ride. I loved the sense of control that I got when I was on top. Smacking sounds filled the air as my ass collided with his pelvis.

"Fuckkk! It's so good, baby. You gonna make me cum," I cried out.

Sticking his tongue out, he reached up to grab my neck. Wrapping my tongue around his, we engaged in a nasty kiss, and I rode him until he filled me up with more of his seeds.

"I swear you keep fuckin me like that, you gon' be the definition of barefoot and pregnant."

I held the hand up with my new eye candy. "As long as I got

this, you can get all the babies you want, sir." I felt him harden beneath me and smiled.

"And just like that, we got action."

We made love again, this time with me on my side. Thankfully, the couch was spacious enough for such activity. Once we were good and tired out, we fell asleep under the glow of the Christmas lights from our tree. I don't think I could've prayed for a better man.

Charisma

Today was the day of our family Christmas Eve brunch, and my mother requested that we wear white and different shades of blue in honor of my father. Blue was his favorite color, and it filled his wardrobe when he was here. I chose a pair of white flared pants and a blue silk shirt. The night before, I'd stayed on the phone with my mother for nearly two hours, reminiscing about Dad and making sure she felt good about going through with today. I wanted to make sure that her heart could bear the celebration of family and remembrance.

"You sure you ready for tomorrow, Ma?"

She let out a soft sigh. "I prayed about it, and I'm ready. I'm getting all my strength through your dad as we speak. And there's no better time than now with his baby about to have a baby of her own."

I went silent, letting her words linger. I was set to give birth any day now, and my dad not being here to witness it made my heart hurt. I didn't express the hurt often to my mom. I always wanted to consider her loss. While I lost a father, she lost the love of her life. Though we both felt the pain, we were grieving differently, and I wanted to remain mindful of that.

"I miss him so much, Mommy. I wish he could've been here to see all of this happen, ya know?"

"He's here, boo. He's been here in spirit. I like to think that he's up there with Hasan's dad, watching the two of you like, how the hell did this happen?" We both laughed. "It's gonna be a great day tomorrow. Filled with love, laughter, and Daddy's presence."

"I know. I love you, Mommy."

"I love you too, daughter."

Hasan entered the room with a reassuring smile on his face and my Stanley cup in his hand. "Here you go. You ready to head out?"

I nodded. "I have a feeling today is gonna be a hard day for me."

Kissing my forehead, he pulled a piece of hair behind my ear. I'd opted to do my own hair for the brunch with his assistance of course. He'd learned his way around a blow dryer and a flat iron the last couple months.

"We're gonna do our best to see to it that it isn't. You'll be surrounded by your people, so the moment you feel sad, remember that this day was special to your pops, and he would've wanted the family together in his absence."

"Your parents did a good job raising you."

"You gotta throw Unc in there too. If it wasn't for him stressing the importance of me turning my savage down a little, I don't know if you'd like the man that stood before you."

"Shoutout to Unc too. Are we picking up Bells on our way there? Ooh." I let up, grabbing my stomach.

"What? You good?"

"Yeah. Look, the little gymnast is in there tumbling around." I pointed to my stomach just in time to see the baby moving about.

"That shit so wild. Are you hurting?"

"No. Just discomfort. Once she gets in her position, it'll pass."

"Okay. And no, since Bella will be with us Christmas day, she'll be with Heather tonight."

"Ooookay. That makes sense. I'm ready."

Holding out his hand for me to take, we descended the steps, grabbed our coats, and headed out the door. The cool air hit my face, and I felt my dad's presence. As if he knew I needed him, a sense of calm came over me. I knew today would be an emotional one, but I felt an easiness in knowing his spirit would engulf the restaurant as we celebrated.

THE RIDE to the restaurant was filled with periods of reflective silence as Tamar Braxton's Christmas album played on a low volume. When we arrived, the decorative blue and white balloon arch gave way to the festivities inside. If I knew anything, I knew my mother was gonna do it big, if not bigger, after our hiatus. Reaching the front door, the smell of freshly baked pastries mingled in the air. I put my hand up to push the door open, but it didn't budge.

"That's odd. Why would the door be locked?" I asked out loud.

"That's weird," Hasan said. "You think she's still working on putting everything together?"

"Bae, you know my mom don't do late." Checking my purse for the restaurant key, I sucked my teeth, realizing that I'd left my keys on the dresser. "I don't have..."

"It's open. I texted Ma."

Turning my head slightly toward him, I pursed my lips. "What's going on?"

With a straight face, he replied, "Christmas brunch. Open the door, bae. It's cold out here."

Skeptically pushing the door open, I was taken aback by the Winter Wonderland themed dining area. The transformation was breathtaking. The room sparkled under twinkling lights draped from the ceiling, casting a glow over the entire place. The tables spread throughout were draped in crisp white linens with silver runners and centerpieces made of crystal vases with white rose arrangements. The glitter sprinkled on the pedals gave it a nice touch.

"Mommy did her thing."

"Yeah, she did. She said everyone entered through the back in the private room. She wanted to surprise everyone with the setup."

"Well, she sure surprised me." I laughed. "I'm excited to see everyone. Come on." Trying to move faster than my belly would allow, I pulled Hasan toward the back room that my mother sometimes rented out for parties.

Pushing the side door open, the family shouted, "Merry Christmas Eve!"

My eyes scanned the room, and I quickly realized that they had gotten me again. The room was decorated similarly to the dining area, only this one was clearly fit for a baby shower.

"Y'all gotta stop! Merry Christmas Eve, family!"

I made my way through the sea of family and friends, giving hugs and kisses, trying my best not to pick up my little cousins that I hadn't seen in a while. Reaching the front of the room, I spotted my mother, Asani, and Brae'lynn all bright eyed and bushy tailed.

"Always up to something. I thought we agreed that we wouldn't have a baby shower?" The way the packages had been coming in by the boatload from all of the things my mother and Hasan had ordered, I didn't see a need for a shower.

"This is true," my mother stated. "We did agree to that, but your husband-to-be wouldn't have it."

"At all," I heard Hasan say from behind me as he wrapped his arms around my waist and kissed the back of my neck. "My princess deserves to be celebrated."

"Yeah. That's what I said, bro." Brae'lynn agreed, patting Hasan on the back. "Now, let's get on with the festivities. I'm in charge of games, and I wanna goat on how creative I was in picking them."

"Okay, before we do that, let's just establish that I'm considered the winner by default for every game because I'm the mommy to be."

They each looked at each other before sharing a laugh.

"Who said that?" Brae'lynn let out. "What baby shower handbook is that in, boo?"

"You my winner, Ma. You never lose with me," Hasan said all cute and shit, making me blush.

"I love how you lie with a sweet face," my mother chimed in. "You're gonna make a great husband. Let the games begin."

And just like that, the surprise elements of the day unfolded. "What You Feedin' My Baby?" was the first game, and to start it off, me and Hasan were blindfolded and fed various spoonfuls of baby food, each one being nastier than the others in my opinion. By the time we made it to the last jar, I questioned if it was even real food they were feeding us. The crowd found it hysterical once I pulled off the blindfold and realized it was indeed pureed baby food. After swearing to Hasan that I would commit my time to ensuring that I prepared our baby's jar foods once she was ready, we were on to the next game.

"Diaper Duty" had me in tears as I watched the men frantically race to see who could change the diaper on a Baby Alive that Brae'lynn had provided in under a minute. When it got down to Hasan and his uncle, my man was declared the winner. I cheered him on as he held up his work with pride.

"That's my man! Go, baby!"

The crowd got a kick out of us. The games continued with

two rounds of "Baby Bingo", "Name That Baby Tune", and "Guess The Size Of The Bump". I had to give it to Brae'lynn. She picked the best games that kept everyone engaged. After handing out the gifts to the winners, including myself, again by default, we all sat down to eat. The spread of fried chicken, Belgian waffles, shrimp and grits, handmade honey buttered biscuits, and a plethora of other foods was divine. As I looked over the room, I became emotional. Everyone was in attendance, just as they had been the previous years when my father was alive.

"Can I have everyone's attention please?" my mother requested as she stood from her seat. All chatter ceased to give her the floor. "I want to say thank you to each and every one of you for coming out on such short notice. Not only are we here to celebrate Christmas but to celebrate my first gran who's about to make her debut sooner than we think. We're also gathered to ce..." She paused, her emotions getting the best of her, causing me to tear up.

Grabbing her hand, I gave it a light squeeze. "It's okay, Mommy. I got you." I assured her just as Hasan had done me before leaving the house.

"We're also gathered here in honor of the love of my life. Bringing the family together on Christmas day was Dre's favorite thing to do. I appreciate all of you for giving me and Charisma the time we needed to grieve. And while I miss him more and more each day, I feel his spirit with me from the time I wake up until the time I close my eyes at night, and that's a blessing within itself. I know he's watching over us at this very moment and smiling big at his baby girl having her own baby girl. That said, I'd like to give you the first gift before we get to the others." Reaching under the table, she pulled out a gift bag. "Daddy would've wanted you to have this," she said, handing me a book.

I recognized it as the memory book she'd started for me and my dad from the day I was born. Inside were a plethora of pictures of he and I with handwritten notes by him with the time, date, and how he felt in those moments. Standing, I threw my arms around her, overwhelmed by her love. Just when I thought my heart couldn't take anymore, Hasan directed everyone's attention to the large screen set up in the corner of the room. The lights dimmed, and a video began to play, showcasing family photos and videos of my dad.

When it ended, my face was flushed with tears, remembering his smile and how much he loved me. Hearing his voice and signature laugh did my heart good, as I hadn't heard it in so long. Slowly, the room lit back up once the video ended. There wasn't a dry eye in the building. My dad was everything.

With everyone good and full, we ended the night with Hasan and I opening half the gifts. There was no way I could get through them all. Big Mama was tired, so tired that I slept the whole way home with Hasan having to nudge me awake once we arrived.

"You held it down today, baby. Your dad's presence was really felt."

"I couldn't have done it without you," I whispered,

cuddling up to him on the couch where we decided to end our night. "I could never thank you enough."

Lifting my head by my chin, he kissed my lips. "You're my world. You know that."

"Mmmhmm. I know, baby. You sleepy?"

He chuckled. "No, but you are. Go to sleep. We got a big day ahead of us tomorrow. Bella is about to go to work on all those presents under the tree."

"Don't I know it." I laughed along with him. "I love you, handsome."

"I love you more, beautiful." Closing my eyes, I settled into a peaceful slumber.

Hasan

I awoke early on Christmas morning to Charisma nestled in my arms, cradling her belly lovingly. Today, we were taking it easy and celebrating our first Christmas as a new family. We had plans to bake cookies with Bella, make gingerbread houses, and open gifts in our matching pjs. A nigga really made it to matching pjs. Yeah, I'd stepped into grown man status. With her sound asleep, I figured this would be the best time to grab the gifts I'd been hiding from her inside of the laundry room.

Carefully, I shifted, trying not to disturb her too much. I couldn't get my arm from under her head good enough before her eyes blinked open. A slow smile spread across her face as she looked up at me.

"What are you up to, Hasan?" she questioned, her voice still thick with sleep.

"Nothing. Merry Christmas, baby." I kissed her forehead and then her nose.

"Mmmm, Merry Christmas." Stroking her belly, she yawned.

"You ready to get the day started? Or you wanna go get in the bed and catch a few more zzzzs?"

Sitting up straight, she nodded. "I'm ready to get the day started. I think I slept enough."

"Okay, you want me to make breakfast, or you wanna stop and get something once we head out to get Bells? I figured we'd pick her up early, so we can make the most out of the day. I also wanted to stop by my mom's place to drop off her gifts."

"I'll skip breakfast, but if you're hungry, I can whip you up something real quick."

Standing up in front of her, I pulled her to her feet. "Skipping breakfast wasn't an option, love. You don't have to have anything heavy but put something on your stomach so that you're not nauseous during the car ride."

"Okay, I can do that." she replied without a fight.

We made our way to the kitchen where I fixed her up a fruit medley of strawberries and blueberries with honey drizzled over the top. I made myself a bowl of cereal and stood at the kitchen island while she sat at the table.

"Bae, where we gonna put all that stuff that we got yesterday? They went crazy. I know we have double of a couple things." Scooping a spoonful of fruit into her mouth, she chewed it slowly, unaware of how hard my dick was just watching her work her jaw.

"We'll have to go through everything and see. Not today though. Today, we're just chilling. No events, no surprises, just gifts and Christmasy stuff."

"You sure?"

Chuckling, I held my hand up. "I swear."

"Alright. Here, come and taste this fruit."

"You gon' put it on the counter, baby?"

"Put wha..." Catching onto my sexual innuendo, she smirked and glanced down at her stomach. "I don't think I can get up there with all this belly."

Up for the challenge, I tapped the island. "You wanna give it a try? I think we can make something shake."

Always willing to please, she stood from the chair, unclasped her bra, and let it slide down her arms to the floor. Turning so that her back was facing me, she slid her panties off slowly. Licking my lips in anticipation, I sat my bowl down and walked around the island to get a better view. Placing one hand on the table and the other on the chair to steady herself, she made her left cheek jump.

"The counter may not be safe but will this work?"

"Hell yeah!"

Stepping out of my boxers, I stroked my dick as I took the few steps toward her. Placing the tip at her opening, I reached up, grabbing a handful of titty while filling her up inch by inch.

"Sssss, don't squeeze them, baby. They sore," she said, referring to her nipples.

"I'm sorry," I whispered in her ear before kissing her neck.

"Mmm, it's okay," she moaned. "It feels so good."

"Daddy always wanna make you feel good, baby. No pain. I love you so much, girl. Even at nine months pregnant, you taking that dick so good."

I stroked in and out of her at a slow pace, trying to fight back the urge to bust. The way her pussy muscles wrapped around my dick made me wanna propose again.

"You gon' always take this dick, 2A?"

"Yessss," she let out in a passion filled tone.

"Tell me you gon' always take this dick." Turning slightly so that I had direct access to her g-spot, I hit it with precision.

"I'ma... oouuu, fuck... I'ma always take this dick. Ughhhh, I'ma cum."

"Damn, you so wet. Go head and let it go." I grabbed a hold of her waist and sped up my strokes.

"Yessss, right there. I'm cummin'!" Her body shook as she held on tightly to the chair. And as she rained down on me, I followed suit, pumping her full of cum.

"Damn, I felt that shit in my toes."

She giggled. "You gotta help me. It's drippin' down my leg."

Easing out of her wetness, my dick was coated with her essence. "That pussy don't be fuckin' around."

"You just say anything." She blushed, picking up her panties and bra from the floor. "We gotta shower, so we can go get my baby."

"Can I get you again in there?"

"If I let you in again, we'll never leave this house, and you know it. Hold me to it later?"

Slapping her ass, I squeezed the left cheek. "You know I will."

Following behind her into the bathroom, I set the shower to a temperature that accommodated both of us. While I was cool with a hot shower, she always had the temperature set to hell. Showers together were a form of intimacy that she loved, and whenever she requested it, I let her know that if she had it set to second degree burn, she could count me out.

"Bella is gonna lose it when she sees all the stuff she got," Charisma commented.

"Yeah. I can't wait for her to see that Barbie Benz." Gently washing her back, I kneeled down to get her legs.

"How you think she's gonna feel not spending the day wit you and her mom like she usually does?"

Standing, I shrugged. "She's only three, bae. She ain't thinkin' bout none of that. Trust me. Here, let me get around you." I went to move her, and she stiffened slightly before gasping. "What's wrong?"

She clutched her stomach and lowered her head. Just then, I noticed water dripping down her legs like she was peeing.

"Pissin' in the shower is crazy, bae," I joked, hoping the clear liquid wasn't what I thought it was.

"No, bae, my water just broke," she said calmly with a mixture of excitement and fear in her eyes.

"Shit, you sure?" I asked, turning the shower off.

"Yes, I'm sure."

"Okay, come on. Take your time."

Helping her out of the shower, I dried her off and got her

into a sweatsuit. Throwing on a sweatsuit of my own, I listened carefully as she instructed me on what she wanted to add to the hospital bag she'd packed and repacked three times while she called Dr. Clarke. Once she was satisfied with the contents of the bag, we made our way out the house and in the car. She appeared cool, calm, and collected, but I could tell that she was starting to feel the contractions by the way she squeezed her eyes shut every few minutes and hit the door.

"Hold my hand, bae. I got you." I instructed and assured her at the same time.

With the assistance of Siri, I started making calls. First, I called her mother, then her best friends, and finally my mother. I made sure to make each call brief but with the same amount of urgency and the same script, "Charisma's water just broke, meet us at the hospital. Drive safe." We pulled up to the emergency room entrance and were met by the same nurse that greeted us days prior when she had the false alarm.

"Back so soon?" She smiled, guiding Riz into the wheelchair she'd rolled out with her.

"Yeah. Sssss, ouuu, wait, don't push yet," Riz said with her hand out, and I assumed she was working through a contraction.

"Whatever you need, honey," the nurse said in a calm tone.

"Mmmm, okay." She took deep breaths in and out. "I'm ready."

"Me too, baby."

The nurse wheeled her inside, and I kept up the pace,

holding her hand. I was about to watch the love of my life bring life into this world. It would be a Merry Christmas indeed.

"HEY, WHERE ARE YOU?" Heather questioned as soon as the call connected.

At Charisma's suggestion, I'd called Heather after the doctor had come in to check her cervix. By the time our mothers, Brae'lynn, and Asani made it, she was already eight centimeters dilated. And according to Dr. Clarke, she didn't see Charisma being in labor too long. Though I didn't want to leave her side to make the call, I did anyway.

"I'm at the hospital with Charisma. She's in labor."

"Oh, does that mean you're not coming to get Bella?"

"To sit in the hospital for hours on Christmas day? No, Heather, I'm not. I just wanted to call you and give you a heads up."

Peeking into the room, I could see the ladies surrounding Charisma and could hear words of encouragement. Our village was on it.

"It kinda sucks that this is happening on Christmas day. I know you were looking forward to having Bella with you. It's cool though. She can unwrap the rest of the gifts here and see you when you leave the hospital, I guess."

Pinching the bridge of my nose, I reminded myself of where I was and what was about to happen in just a few short hours.

"Can you put my baby on the phone?"

"Yeah, I was..."

"Bella, Heather. Just put Bella on the phone please."

Sucking her teeth, she called out to Bells whose voice I could hear a few seconds later. Switching the audio call to Face-Time, she appeared on the screen, dressed in her pajamas.

"Daddy!" she yelled excitedly.

"Merry Christmas, Daddy baby."

"Daddy, come." She spoke clearly, taking the phone from Heather and walking away. "Thassa tree." She pointed out, holding the phone up to the top of the tree where the star was.

I laughed. "That's a nice tree, pretty girl. Guess what?"

I could see Heather's hand as she fixed the phone so that it was back on Bells' face.

"Daddy."

"Bells, Risma is having your baby today," I said to which she just smiled. "Daddy gonna pick you up later, so you can see the baby, okay?"

She nodded as if she understood, and that was fine with me.

"Do you know what time you'll be here?" Heather inquired, taking the phone.

"Hey," Asani peeked her head out of the room, "she said she feels like she needs to push. You might wanna get in here."

"Okay. Heather, I gotta go. I'll call when I'm on my way to get her."

Ending the call before she could say anything else, I went back to the room to be by Charisma's side. Dr. Clarke entered right behind me. Figuring they must've informed her too, I felt my adrenaline start to rush.

"Okay, Charisma, we can only have two people in the room for delivery. I need you to call them out, so we can get them gowned and gloved up."

"My... ooouuu wait..." She squeezed my hand as a contraction passed, doing her best to breathe through it. "My mom and my fiancé."

"We'll be out in the waiting room," my mother said, kissing my cheek and then Charisma's. "It sucks being the boy mom," she joked, as she passed Ms. Cheryl. "You got this, Grandma."

"For the both of us," Ms. Cheryl assured.

"Love youuuu," Brae'lynn and Asani sang as they headed to the door.

"I love y'all too. We're having a baby!" Charisma cheered, and the trio did some dance that had the doctor and her two nurses laughing.

Me and Ms. Cheryl were gowned and gloved then back at her side. I recognized the glint of uncertainty in her eyes that she did her best to cover with a smile. Taking her hand in mine, I kissed the back of it.

"I got you. You hear me?"

She nodded.

"Say we got this," I coached, tuning out everyone in the room.

Taking a deep breath in and slowly breathing out, she repeated, "We got this."

"Aight. Gimmie my princess, 2A."

Charisma

Here we were, at the finish line and ready to do a thing. Gone were the Braxton Hicks contractions. This was the real thing, and it hurt like hell. I didn't know who told me I was God's strongest soldier when I proudly refused that epidural, but I had for sure played myself. Even Hasan's encouraging words, although soothing, wasn't enough to fight the pressure and pain I felt in my coochie.

"Oh, my Goddd!!! It hurts!" I screamed out after the second push.

"She's almost here, boo," my mother informed as she held my hand.

"Well, tell her to come on!"

"She's coming, Charisma. I need you to push for me again,

sweetie," Dr. Clarke said. She was at the foot of the bed calm and focused, similar to Hasan.

Every time I looked up at him, he gave me reassuring eyes and a head nod. "We're almost there."

"Okay, we're gonna push on three," Dr. Clarke announced before counting.

When she got to three, I pushed with all I had in me, and I felt her come through before her perfect cry filled the room. Tears streamed down my face as Dr. Clarke held our baby up in the air like Simba in *The Lion King* before handing her over to me.

"Congratulations, Mom."

Even covered in amniotic fluid, she was the most perfect baby I'd ever seen. I knew they had to clean her up, but I just wanted to hold her close and never let her go.

"You did it," my mother whispered, kissing my forehead. "You did it."

I closed my eyes to relish in the moment and opened them to meet Hasan's.

"We need to..."

"Give her a name," he finished my sentence for me. His lips pulled into the smile that I loved so much. "I know."

We'd done the second round of name picking the day after the false labor. We were down to three, with Ocean still on the table because I was in love with the name. I also liked the other two names but wanted us to come to a decision together. She needed a name fitting for how perfect she was.

"Tru," I breathed out what resonated the most.

"Tru Ocean Mackley." He winked. "You give a little; I give a little."

"I love you." Puckering my lips, he kissed them.

"I love you too, baby."

"Alright, Mommy and Daddy. You mind if we take the little one, so we can clean her off?" the nurse asked.

"Yeah, give them the baby so I can hold her," my mom chimed in, making the nurse laugh.

Parting with Tru, I gave the signal for Hasan to follow. We'd already discussed that wherever the baby went, he went until I was up and moving. I'd watched more than enough documentaries of children being kidnapped from the safest places. No way was anyone getting mine. While she was cleaned up, the other nurse helped me get situated and covered.

After a few minutes, Tru was placed back in Hasan's arms then transferred over to my mom.

"I'm gonna go out and let everyone know the princess is here," Hasan said.

"Okay."

"Look who finally made it out to see Gran," my mother whispered. Her voice was a low whisper of love and joy. "You know, I've been waiting for you to come and see me. I have so many stories to tell you."

"I hope none of those stories include any of my embarrassing moments." I laughed lightly.

"Nahhh, I'm gonna show you in the best light. She's so

beautiful, Charisma. You did so well." I could see the weight of her new title settling in, as she held Tru close, swaying from side to side.

Tru began to whimper, and her gentle shushing reminded me of when I was little. I thought about my dad and how he would've reacted to seeing her.

"I wish Dad was here to see her," I said softly. My voice conveyed the heaviness I felt for his absence at such a pivotal moment in my life.

My mother's gaze met mine, understanding and empathizing with me. I could see she was holding back tears. "He's here. He made sure his favorite girl brought the newest blessing in on his favorite holiday. If that isn't a testament to his presence, I don't know what is."

I smiled, wiping the tears that had fallen down my cheeks. "You're right."

"Knock, knock," Hasan's mom said, peeking her head inside the door. "Is there room for another grandma and the aunties?"

"Yes, of course," I confirmed.

The three of them stumbled in with Hasan lagging behind. The room was filled with awwws and oh, my Gods as they fawned over Tru. When it was time to choose who would hold her first, neither one could figure it out, so Brae'lynn came up with the bright idea of three rounds of Rock, Paper, Scissors to settle it.

"While y'all figure that out, I'm gonna go head and get my

time in," Ms. Gladys said, washing her hands at the sink in the room.

"Somebody put the timer on," Brae'lynn let out, and we laughed.

"Don't worry bout the timer. You'll be holding her last." Asani snickered. "Come on, rock, paper, scissors says shoot."

Hasan walked back over to me and sat on the edge of the bed. "Yo, they crazy."

"I know." I chuckled. "You gon' let them hog yo' baby?"

"Nahhh, I wanna give everyone their time before I clear the room."

"Well, that's very nice of you. You checked in with Bells?"

"Yeah. I was thinking about going to get her, so she can come and see the baby. What you think?"

"I'd love that. Can I have a hug?"

He nodded and pulled me into his embrace. "I'd say this will go down in the books as the best Christmas I've ever had."

"I had a baby on my dad's favorite holiday. Nothing can top that."

Later in the evening, as visiting hours came to a close, our family reluctantly said their goodbyes to baby Tru. With Ms. Gladys convincing Hasan to let Bella stay the night at her house, it was just us again. Me, Hasan, and our new addition. As Tru lay on my chest, I traced the contours of her round face, marveling at the little human that was a product of the love Hasan and I shared. Her small cooing sounds were a new sound that I had already committed to memory. Glancing down, I saw a glint of my engagement ring and smiled. Babyface had come in and completely reshaped my life.

"What you thinking about?" he asked, leaning over the foot of the bed.

"Us and how real this is. You were just stalking me last summer."

He laughed. "Don't go telling our baby that lie when you tell her the story of how we met."

"What? I gotta tell Tru the truth. Out of all the doors you could've slammed that man up against, you chose mine. And then you ran me down those other times."

Shaking his head, he positioned himself on the other side of the small hospital bed. "Tru, Daddy gonna teach you your first word right now. It's CAP. C... A...P..." He spelled out the words. "It's when someone lies about something, and you know it's a lie, so you call them on it. Mommy's cappin' right now. Now, it doesn't make her a bad mommy. A cap ass mommy, yes, but not a bad one."

Releasing a small laugh, I yawned. "Daddy silly, Tru." My eyelids felt heavy, a sign that the long day had caught up with me. "Can you..."

"I got her," he responded, in tune with me. "Rest up, we have a lifetime to enjoy our little one."

Content in knowing that, I let my eyes close for much needed rest. I'd pushed out a seven-pound baby, epidural free. It was safe to say that I deserved a few naps and a bottle of Don, Don, Don Juliooooo.

THE NEXT TWO days in the hospital went by quick. Between the newborn checks, new mommy checks, and just the ongoing movement, I was ready to get back to the quietness of my home. Today was the day. Donned in her First Day Out onesie and fully layered, Tru was ready to roll. However, her dad insisted that he do his own car seat check behind the nurse.

I sat on the bed watching Hasan meticulously check the straps on the car seat, making sure every buckle and strap were just right. When he was satisfied, he picked Tru up from the bed, pecked her cheek, and carefully strapped her in. Funny how he wanted to reproof a car seat that we'd purchased. Sitting back, I let him do his thing.

"Gotta make sure this thing is Daddy approved. You ready, bae?"

"Yep." Grabbing my premade hospital bag and the diaper bag full of baby stuff my mother forced me to steal, I started out behind him. I'd opted out of the wheelchair offered to me, ready to fall right back into the Ms. Independent role immediately.

Walking through the halls of labor and delivery, we ran into Dr. Clarke on our way to the elevators.

"Look at you moving about without that extra dip in your step," she commented, hugging me.

"You mean my waddle?" I replied lightheartedly.

"Yeah, that." She laughed. "Congratulations again,

Charisma. I'll see you in six weeks for your checkup." She cut her eye at a grinning Hasan when she mentioned the six weeks.

"I'll see you then and thank you."

"My pleasure and drive safe."

Getting on the elevator, Hasan turned to me. "You know I gotta see about you before that six week check up, right?"

"Your birthday is just before that time, so you betta do it like it's yo bday, do it like it's yo bday, babyyy." I twisted my hips, reciting Joseline Hernandez's lyrics.

"I can see you now, pregnant again."

Repeating Joseline's lyrics as the elevator doors opened to the lobby, I gave the nonverbal go ahead for him to shoot my club up if he saw fit. Yeah, he had it like that.

Back home, we walked in the door, and I was met with the smell of fresh linens. Hasan had given our mothers a key to our place at their request so that they could freshen up the place before our arrival, one of the many sweet gestures I knew was to come. I looked over at the tree where the gifts still sat, stacked neatly underneath it.

"We gotta give Bella a Christmas do over, bae. She didn't even get to open her gifts."

"Yeah, I know. But, trust me, she didn't miss out on anything. Between her mom, my mom, Unc, and Liv, she got more than enough. We'll have her open everything here tomorrow when I pick her up. Let's get the two of you settled. My baby bout to start it up if I don't get this snowsuit off her."

"Okay. I'm gonna go shower. You need me to do anything?"

"Other than exist, be a great mother to our girls, and fuck me like you weren't raised right, nah."

"Be a woman, a mother, and a whore, got it."

"Tru, your mother is a genius. I love you, woman."

"I love you back, Babyface."

As I made my way upstairs, I couldn't help but feel that everything leading up to now was exactly the way it was meant to be. God had blessed me with my soulmate and then doubled down, blessing my womb to further show a reflection of the love we shared. I couldn't call it luck; this was **fate**.

Epilogue

HASAN

"Looking at all this land, damn I used to be a lonely man. Could never understand why I had no one to take my hand. But then the weather changed, Mother Nature brought the sun my way. Now, girl, you're who I am. And I have you for the rest of my days."

R. Kelly's *Forever More* played as Charisma walked down the aisle in a form fitting, cream colored dress to meet me. Her hair was pinned up, displaying her beautiful face that held a smile so big you could tell she was being loved properly. True to my word, I took my uncle's advice, and today, we were standing before our family and friends, officially committing ourselves to one another. We were a month into parenthood, and Tru was growing leaps and bounds. I didn't see a reason for us to wait any longer when I knew the moment I put the ring on her finger that I wanted her to be my wife. One conversation about a wedding during a night feeding turned into wedding plans the next day.

And as I watched my future take steps toward me, I looked out into the small crowd that filled the ceremony space. Bella sat on my mother's lap after having been the prettiest flower girl ever, and Ms. Cheryl sat next to her, holding a sleeping Tru. The setting was intimate, just as Charisma requested. Stopping at the end of the aisle, she swapped bouquets with Asani, who gave her a thumbs up. Finally making it to me, she reached for my hand, and the officiant started.

Going over his rehearsed wedding spiel, he called for each of us to read our vows. Charisma went first.

"I didn't write anything down because I knew I'd be a mess by the second sentence so bear with me, family. Hasan, as I stand here before you, every bit of the woman I always knew I'd be, I want you to know that you being by my side only makes me better. Thank you for always putting me first and allowing me to flourish in my femininity. I never have to worry about you showing up because wherever I am, there you are. You're my backpack, baby."

I chuckled, and the crowd laughed. Holding the bouquet up, she continued. "As we celebrate our union, there are two people I know we would've loved to be here today. Two men that we hold close, that I'm positive were instrumental in us meeting the way we did." Tilting the bouquet so that I could see the top of it, I squeezed my eyes shut. Two pictures of our dads were somehow placed strategically in the roses. "It wouldn't have been right if I didn't have our fathers walk us down the aisle."

Temporarily forgetting about the normal order of things, I pulled her to me and buried my face in her neck. "I love you," I whispered, getting choked up.

"I love you so much," she replied, heartfelt.

Stepping back, I let out an emotion filled sigh. I had to pull it together to recite my vows. "I had something written down, but after this, it's gonna sound corny," I joked to keep myself from tears. "You are a woman after my own heart. Cut from a fabric of your own. You make it easy to show up every single day, and it does my heart good to know that you know that our family is in able hands. Today, I vow to continue to be the man that my father raised and show your father everyday why he can rest easy knowing **I** got you. And you'll forever remain wrapped in my love."

I DON'T WANNA ARGUE!

HAPPY HOLIDAYS, BOOKA

Review

Did you enjoy the read?
Let us know how much by leaving us a review on Amazon and
Goodreads

Snatched Up By A Hitta

Santa Sent Me A Real One For Christmas

Wet Dreams On Lockdown: The Unit Manager

Thug Me The Right Way

Thug Me The Right Way 2

Thug Me The Right Way 3

Seizing A Gangsta's Heart For The Summer

Yours For The Taking

Other Books By

<u>URBAN AINT DEAD</u>

Tales 4rm Da Dale

The Hottest Summer Ever

Hittin' Licks For The Holidays: Atlanta

Wet Dreams On Lockdown: The Nurse

How To Publish A Book From Prison

By **Elijah R. Freeman**

Despite The Odds

By **Juhnell Morgan**

Good Girls Gone Rogue

Good Girls Gone Rogue 2

By **Manny Black**

Hittaz

Hittaz 2

Hittaz 3

Hittaz 4

Hittaz 5

Coldhearted

The State's Witness

The State's Witness 2

The State's Witness 3

This Time Won't You Save Me

This Time Won't You Save Me 2

His Summer Side Piece

By **Kyiris Ashley**

Stuck In The Trenches

Stuck In The Trenches 2

By **Huff Tha Great**

Melted the Heart of a Menace

Wet Dreams On Lockdown: Lieutenant Grace

By P. Wise

Merry Trapmas: Ice & Frost

By **Mia Sky**

Thug Me The Right Way

By **DiamondATL & Nai**

Atlantastan

Atlantastan 2

By **Chris Green**

IN The Streetz

IN The Streetz 2

IN The Streetz 3

By **Tron Hill**

Hittin' Licks for the Holidays: New York

By **Freshh Moneyy**

Wet Dreams on Lockdown: The Male C.O

By **Tamyra Griffin**

Wet Dreams On Lockdown: The Counselor

By **Paris Iman**

Wet Dreams On Lockdown: The Warden

By **Shawnice**

Wet Dreams On Lockdown: The Captain

By **TN Jones**

Books By

URBAN AINT DEAD's C.E.O

<u>Elijah R. Freeman</u>

Triggadale

Triggadale 2

Triggadale 3

Tales 4rm Da Dale

The Hottest Summer Ever

Murda Was The Case

Murda Was The Case 2

Murda Was The Case 3

Hittin' Licks For The Holidays: Atlanta

Wet Dreams On Lockdown: The Nurse

How To Publish A Book From Prison

Stay Connected

Follow
Elijah R. Freeman
On Social Media
FB: Elijah R. Freeman
IG: @the_future_of_urban_fiction